The Vet

by Susan Hartley • illustrated by Anita DuFalla

Sam said, "I have to go to Val the vet. I want to see if Tim is well. Do you want to go with me?"

Pop said, "Tan cat,
you do not look well.
You look fat. You and I will
go to the vet with Sam."

Pop and Sam put Tim
and the fat cat in the van.
They went to the vet.

Vin said, "Are you
here to see Val?"
"Yes," said Pop and Sam.
"Come in," said Val the vet.

"Tim is well," said Val.
"And yes, the cat is fat,
but she is well. Go home and
put the cat in a bed."

Pop and Sam went home
with Tim and the fat tan cat.
Pop put the fat cat in a bed.

"Look at my cat.
She is not fat now!"